For my parents, who filled my childhood with books, crayons and encouragement

London Borough of Richmond Upon Thames	
RTK	
90710 000 387 463	
Askews & Holts	
JF	£6.99
	9781786281838

First published in 2019 by Child's Play (International) Ltd
Ashworth Road, Bridgemead, Swindon SN5 7YD, UK

Published in USA by Child's Play Inc
250 Minot Avenue, Auburn, Maine 04210

Distributed in Australia by Child's Play Australia Pty Ltd
Unit 10/20 Narabang Way, Belrose, Sydney, NSW 2085

Copyright © 2019 Phoebe Swan
The moral rights of the author/illustrator have been asserted

All rights reserved

ISBN 978-1-78628-183-8
CLP210818CPL12181838

Printed in Shenzhen, China

1 3 5 7 9 10 8 6 4 2

A catalogue record of this book
is available from the British Library

www.childs-play.com

King
Leonard's
Teddy

Phoebe Swan

King Leonard was very rich. He had everything he could possibly wish for.

If anything broke in his castle, he didn't try to fix it.

He just sent Max to buy a new one!

LION SIZE TV

And he never bothered to clean anything, either.

He only ever used things once, before throwing them straight out of the window!

King Leonard lived quite happily, buying more and more and more stuff!

Until one night, a terrible sound was heard.

King Leonard's beloved teddy,
the one he took to bed
every night, was broken!

"Would you like one of your other teddies, Sir?"

"They're not the same!"

"We could buy you a nice new one?"

"That wouldn't be the same, either!"

"Then you will have to find someone to fix it."

Early the next morning,
King Leonard set off into town.

First, he went to the toy shop.

"Fix your teddy bear? I wouldn't have a clue!
I can sell you a brand new one, though.
Or you could try *throwawayteddies.com*!"

So King Leonard went to the toy factory.

"Fix your teddy bear?
I'm sorry, I can't help you.
We only make new ones."

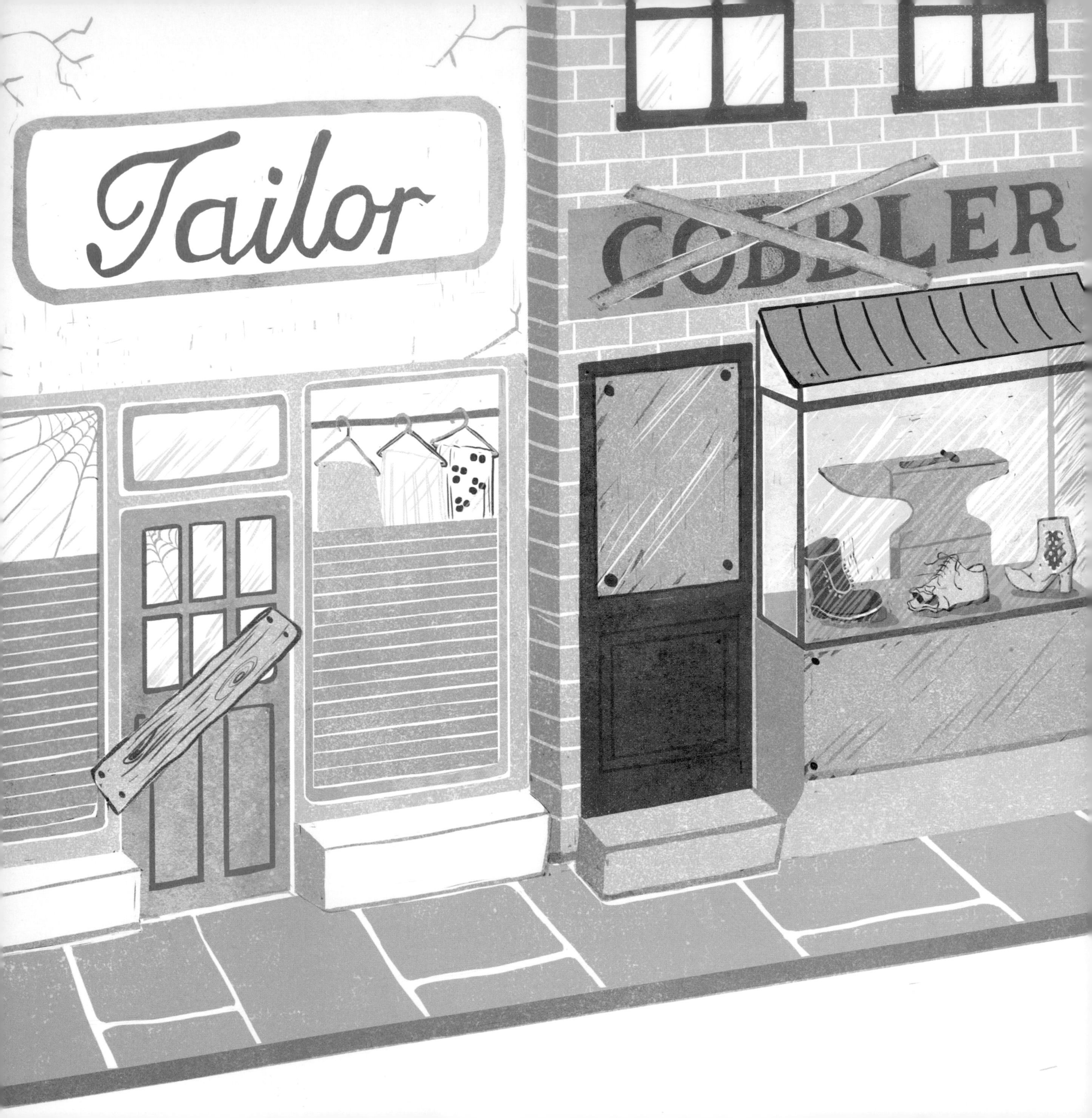
Tailor
COBBLER

King Leonard tried
the old street where
the repair shops used to be,
but they were all boarded up.

Sadly, he headed for home.

Back at his castle, King Leonard was so busy thinking about his teddy that he forgot to look where he was going.

He tripped and fell flat on his face!

Now Teddy was more broken than ever!

"Hey, wait a minute!
There's some string here.
And some stuffing.

Perhaps I can fix Teddy myself!"

King Leonard
got straight to work,
learning how to sew.

HOW TO SEW

It took a few tries...

and lots and lots...

of mistakes...

before he got it right!

Now his teddy was as good as new!

Leonard and Max began to sort through the huge pile of stuff that had been thrown away.

They had a lot of fun fixing things,
or finding new uses for them.

Some things from the pile weren't even broken.
They just needed a good wash, so that they could be used again.

Now that he knew how to repair and reuse things, Leonard realized that he simply didn't need so much stuff. He started to give his belongings away for other people to use.

Word got around. Soon, everyone began to bring their broken things to Leonard, so that he could teach them how they could be fixed.

Once everybody began to waste less and recycle more, Leonard really did have everything he could wish for - and so did everyone else!

Lots of waste we produce is buried underground in landfill sites. This is because it can't be recycled. This waste releases poisons into the water and into the air. It affects the climate and damages plants and animals. Bacteria breaks down most landfill waste, but plastic is a very big problem. It takes hundreds of years to decompose and is difficult to recycle, so we all need to use less.

1 REDUCE

Buy in bulk and refill old containers.

 Say no to plastic straws and cutlery.

Turn the water off when brushing your teeth.

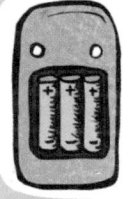 Buy rechargeable batteries.

Save water, refill bottles.

Reduce heating, wear extra clothes.

Use a shopping list, only buy what you need.

Walk or cycle to reduce car journeys.

Use both sides of paper.

Take your own bags when out shopping.

Buy items made from recycled materials.

Use the library.

 Turn the lights off when you leave a room.

 Buy loose fruit and vegetables.

Buy from second-hand shops.

A large amount of food is wasted every year. People buy more food than they can eat, at the supermarkets and in the restaurants. This food could help feed hungry people or be composted to improve the soil, but it is also mostly buried in landfill. We can all try to reduce waste. Here are some ideas to help you and your family make a difference.

2 REUSE

Help wildlife, make a bird feeder.

Reuse newspaper for wrapping up gifts.

3 RECYCLE

 Make your own cards.

Reuse containers for plants.

Compost your food waste.

 Reuse food containers.

Make your own toys and games.

Give clothes to family, friends and charity shops.

Make musical instruments.

Make a greenhouse.

Donate toys and books to local hospitals and playgroups.

 Reuse containers for storage.

Reuse old clothes.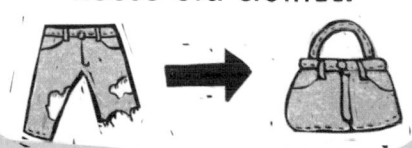

Read labels and sort items into the correct containers.